GROW YOUR MIND

THINK POSITIVE

Written by Alice Harman

Illustrated by David Broadbent

CRABTREE
PUBLISHING COMPANY
WWW.CRABTREEBOOKS.COM

CRABTREE
PUBLISHING COMPANY
WWW.CRABTREEBOOKS.COM

Author: Alice Harman
Series designer: David Broadbent
Illustrator: David Broadbent
Editor: Crystal Sikkens
Proofreader: Melissa Boyce
Print coordinator: Katherine Berti

A trusted adult is a person (over 18 years old) in a child's life who makes them feel safe, comfortable, and supported. It might be a parent, teacher, family friend, social worker, or another adult.

Library and Archives Canada Cataloguing in Publication

Title: Think positive / written by Alice Harman ; illustrated by David Broadbent.
Names: Harman, Alice, author. | Broadbent, David, 1977- illustrator.
Description: Series statement: Grow your mind | Includes index. |
  First published in Great Britain in 2020 by the Watts Publishing Group.
Identifiers: Canadiana (print) 20200222988 |
  Canadiana (ebook) 20200223097 |
  ISBN 9780778781714 (hardcover) |
  ISBN 9780778781790 (softcover) |
  ISBN 9781427125972 (HTML)
Subjects: LCSH: Optimism in children—Juvenile literature. |
  LCSH: Children—Attitudes—Juvenile literature. | LCSH: Optimism—
  Juvenile literature. | LCSH: Attitude (Psychology)—Juvenile literature. |
  LCSH: Well-being—Juvenile literature.
Classification: LCC BF723.O67 H37 2021 | DDC j155.4/18232—dc23

Library of Congress Cataloging-in-Publication Data

Names: Harman, Alice, author. | Broadbent, David, 1977- illustrator.
Title: Think positive / written by Alice Harman ; illustrated by David Broadbent.
Description: New York : Crabtree Publishing Company, 2021. | Series:
  Grow your mind | Includes index.
Identifiers: LCCN 2020015524 (print) |
  LCCN 2020015525 (ebook) |
  ISBN 9780778781714 (hardcover) |
  ISBN 9780778781790 (paperback) |
  ISBN 9781427125972 (ebook)
Subjects: LCSH: Attitude (Psychology)--Juvenile literature. | Optimism--
  Juvenile literature. | Children--Conduct of life--Juvenile literature.
Classification: LCC BF327 .H367 2021 (print) | LCC BF327 (ebook) |
  DDC 155.4/191--dc23
LC record available at https://lccn.loc.gov/2020015524
LC ebook record available at https://lccn.loc.gov/2020015525

Crabtree Publishing Company

www.crabtreebooks.com   1-800-387-7650
Published by Crabtree Publishing Company in 2021

Published in Canada
Crabtree Publishing
616 Welland Ave.
St. Catharines, Ontario
L2M 5V6

Published in the United States
Crabtree Publishing
347 Fifth Ave.
Suite 1402-145
New York, NY 10116

Printed in the U.S.A./082020/CG20200601

First published in Great Britain in 2020 by The Watts Publishing Group Copyright © The Watts Publishing Group 2020

CONTENTS

A positive mindset

Do you think anybody can be happy all the time—never worried, never sad, never angry, scared, or disappointed?

In a way that would be nice, but it's just not realistic! Humans naturally feel all kinds of emotions, and nobody on Earth has felt happy for every single second of their life.

What we can do, though, is train our brains to focus on the good rather than the bad in any situation— even when we're worried or when things don't turn out as we planned.

This helps our brains understand that things really can change for the better, and we have the power to help make that happen.

We often think about our brains as if they are fixed. When we have a **fixed mindset** we believe some people are smart or confident and others aren't. But that's just not true. Your brain is changing all the time, and you can do all kinds of things to help it grow! When we start thinking this way, we are using a **growth mindset**.

You have billions of **neurons** in your brain, which build bridges between themselves to pass around information. The more you have certain thoughts, the stronger those bridges get.

Over time, thinking positively causes your "I can do it!" bridges to get stronger than your "I can't do anything" bridges, so it actually gets easier and easier.

Sounds good, right? Let's get started!

Half full or half empty

Imagine you've just gulped down half a glass of juice. You could think positive and say, "Great, the glass is still half full!" or you could think negative and say, "Oh no, now the glass is half empty!" Either way you look at it, the situation is exactly the same!

When we focus on the negative, such as what we don't have, what we think we can't do, or what could go wrong, the world can seem like quite a scary, unfair place. It can make us feel down and hopeless, so we don't want to do anything.

But by training our brain to look for the positive, we remind it of all the good stuff, such as what we do have, what has gone right, how things can get better, and what we can do about it.

1.
Think about a time when things didn't go quite how you wanted them to. For example, maybe you got into an argument with a friend about something.

3.
On the other side, write down all the positive thoughts and feelings you remember having—there might not be any!

2.
Draw a line down the middle of a sheet of paper to split it into two. On one side, write down all the negative thoughts and feelings you remember having. For example, you might have felt sad and been worried that your friend would stop talking to you.

4.
Now, try to find a positive thought and action for each negative thing you've written down. For example, "I'm worried my friend will stop talking to me" could become "I have a chance to show them how much I care about our friendship, and I can write them a note to tell them that."

All or nothing

It can be easy to think in an "all-or-nothing" way—that a situation is either good or bad, or that you can either do something or you can't.

But this isn't really a helpful or realistic way of thinking. It can make us feel like we might as well not try at all, that things are stuck the way they are and there's no point making any effort to change them.

Instead, try to picture things on a scale from positive to negative. Think about what you can do to push them further toward the "good" or the "I can" end.

Maryam

When my school started a basketball club, I was so excited. At first, it all went really well. I liked my teammates and I was the best at scoring baskets! Everyone started calling me the team's "star player."

Then we played a game against another school. They were really good and I got so nervous that I didn't get in a single shot. We lost by a lot, and even though everyone on my team was really nice, I still felt terrible.

I told my mom I wasn't going to play anymore because I'd let everyone down. But she reminded me that I was part of a team and that my teammates weren't all thinking about me. It's likely they were thinking how they could improve their own performances for the next game.

She also helped me see the positive side of the experience. I had a chance to learn how my nerves could affect my performance. I was also able to see more advanced players in action, which helped me set goals for myself to keep improving.

I'm still on the basketball team and I love it more than ever now!

Celebrate!

Our brains can be pretty impatient sometimes. As soon as we've finished something or finally got the hang of something, they often want to jump ahead to the next thing right away.

But it's important to take a moment to celebrate how hard you've worked! It doesn't just make you feel good, it also makes it easier for your brain to remember it as a positive example of your hard work paying off.

Thinking back over times in the past when you've put in effort and succeeded helps your brain to believe that you can do it again! This can help you feel more positive and confident about facing new challenges.

Try making a "Yes, I can!" list that you can look at whenever you need a positivity boost.

On a sheet of paper, write down two or three examples of times when you found something challenging, but worked really hard to finish it or get better at it.

It could be reading a difficult book, learning how to do a chore at home, talking to new people even though you feel shy—anything you like! Decorate each entry with some gold stars and colored pencils so they all look really special.

Now create a second list—an "I am learning to..." list—and write down things you're working on at the moment. Every time you finish or make progress with something, check it off this list and add it to your "Yes, I can!" list.

You could even say something nice to yourself each time, such as "Well done for putting in so much effort to finish that book, and not giving up when you got frustrated with how tough it was."

Thanks for everything

We can often slip into focusing on what we don't have, rather than all the wonderful things in our lives.

Taking a moment to list everything you're thankful for can make your brain much happier.

You may suddenly find that your worries about what you're missing out on fade away to nothing. Your brain has realized that your life is too full of other things to be thankful for.

Every day for a week, write or draw something that you're grateful for on a scrap of paper. Then drop it in a jar.

It could be anything you like—a tasty dinner, a friend who makes you laugh, a big hug from your mom or dad, your favorite cartoon, a nice teacher, your comfy bed!

At the end of the week, empty the jar and look through all the scraps of paper. You could even close your eyes and imagine yourself surrounded by all these wonderful things!

Keep adding to your jar, and read the scraps of paper whenever you need a reminder of everything you have to be thankful for.

Smile!

Sometimes if you're feeling worried or upset, it can be really hard to think positive. To get in a better mood, a smile or laugh can give your brain a quick positivity boost.

When you smile and laugh, it releases chemicals in your brain, called serotonin and endorphins, that help make you feel happier. Laughing also helps to lower the level of cortisol in your brain. That's a chemical linked to feeling really worried.

But if you're feeling down, how are you supposed to break out into a grin or a giggle?

Here are some ideas to try...

1. Make a bunch of funny, scrunched-up faces and imagine your face turning to jelly between each one! It's a fun way to relax the muscles in your face, which can get tense when you're worried or upset.

2. Think of something that's made you laugh or smile before, such as a cute animal video, a silly joke in a movie, or something funny that your friend said.

3. Watch and listen to other people laughing, whether it's in real life or on a video. Seeing and hearing people laugh can make our brain want us to do the same!

Truly positive

Thinking positively can be really helpful, but it doesn't mean you have to pretend everything is fine when it isn't.

Real positive thinking isn't about ignoring problems, it's about looking for ways to work through them and feel good about yourself and your life.

If something is making you upset or worried, it's always best to talk about it with an adult that you trust, such as a parent or teacher.

Remember, you don't have to handle everything on your own—and no one wants or expects you to try to do that. Sometimes the bravest, most positive thing you can do is to ask for help.

Nerys

Last year, I started finding English class harder and harder. It seemed like all of my friends in class were keeping up fine with the tougher books and activities, but I was too embarrassed to say that I didn't really understand what we were doing.

I started copying answers off the people who sat on either side of me in class. I worried about falling further and further behind over time, but I just tried not to think about that.

Then the teacher gave us some homework to do with one of the books—a kind of diary to fill in over the next couple of weeks, with our own ideas—and I realized that I needed to stop pretending it was all OK.

I spoke to my teacher after class and asked for help. He was really nice about it. Now I know I can always speak up if I get lost, and my dad is helping me with extra reading at home.

17

Let it go

In life, annoying little things just happen sometimes! Drinks get spilled, toys get broken, it rains when you want to go outside...

Rather than letting these things spoil your day by making you angry and upset, try taking a deep breath and letting them go.

Then thank yourself for doing something really good for your brain!

It's happier and works better when you have a positive **attitude**.

Ricardo

What an annoying day! First, a car splashed muddy water on my legs as I walked to school. Then, I realized my mom had given me my brother's lunch box, so I had a sandwich I didn't really like. And last, my friend Laura accidentally broke my favorite pen, which I just lent to her for a second.

It could have turned into the worst day ever. I felt myself getting angry, and I remembered times in the past when I got really annoyed by little things like this.

I snapped at my friends and was rude to my teacher. This just made everything even worse. It also made me feel really bad later on, after I calmed down.

Rather than repeating this again, I just took a deep breath, smiled, and thought "Let it go." It didn't magically stop me from feeling annoyed, but it got easier every time I practiced it. And I felt really good that I made the decision to stay positive.

Feelings detective

Sometimes it's pretty easy to figure out why you're feeling negative about something—why you think you can't do it or don't even want to try it. For example, you might be scared to sign up for gymnastics because you're worried you'll hurt or embarrass yourself.

Other times you might just have a bad feeling and not quite know why. Then it's time to put on your detective hat and try to figure it out!

Once you know what kinds of negative thoughts are going on behind the feeling, you can start figuring out how to deal with each one.

Think of something that makes you feel worried or upset, but you're not quite sure why. Write it down or draw it on a sheet of paper or a notebook page.

Underneath, write the question, "What's the worst that could happen?" Try to answer it, and write down or draw how you think that would make you feel.

It might not feel very nice to think about this, so do this activity with an adult you trust and talk with them about it.

What positive actions can you take so that you feel better about what might happen? Write or draw them, and make a plan with a trusted adult about putting them into practice.

Well done, detective!

Seeing the future

For our brains, sometimes seeing is believing! Using a technique called **visualization** can really help your brain think positive about the future.

Visualization means creating a picture in your mind of something you would like to happen.

We do this because the way our brain works to imagine things and actually take action are linked, and visualization helps our brain think of this positive result as more realistic.

It can give your brain a confidence boost that your goal is possible and worth trying to achieve. But you need to put in effort to actually make it happen!

Draw a picture of something you want to improve at doing. For example, if you play a musical instrument and want to get better at it, you might draw a picture of yourself practicing for 15 minutes every day.

Underneath this picture, write down three steps to help you achieve this. For example, to keep up your musical practice you could:

1. Decide on a set time that you're going to practice every day. Ask an adult to help remind you.

2. Start a practice journal and keep a note of every day you practice.

3. Record yourself playing once a week, so that if you ever feel like skipping practice you can watch and see how much it's helping you improve.

Positive people

Can you think of someone who always tries to see the good in people and look on the bright side of life?

People like this can make us feel really good about ourselves. They can make us believe that we can do anything we put our mind to, and that even if we don't get it right away, it's all going to be OK.

There are others who tend to see things in a negative way. They often complain a lot, thinking everything will turn out badly. They might even put you down. This can really drain your positive energy.

If someone is being very negative and making you feel bad, try talking to them about it. They might not even realize they're doing it!

Sasha

Today was the worst day ever. Everything we had to do in class was really boring and the activities were not fun.

Jonah, who sits next to me, was being so annoying. Neither of us is good at science, but he still kept nagging me to try one of the activities. I finally did, but I couldn't do it so I just gave up.

Jonah

Today was great! Our teacher gave us activities all about wind power and how it can help the planet.

I have to try really hard to understand things in science, so I find it very helpful when we have hands-on activities. I felt like I was really growing my brain today!

I tried hard not to let Sasha's comments get me down, and encouraged her to give an activity a try—and she did! I felt proud of myself for handling that well.

DOING GOOD

Think back to the last time that someone was really kind to you. Maybe they helped you out, said something nice, or listened when you were upset. How does thinking about it make you feel?

When people are kind to us, it can make us think more positive about ourselves and the world. That makes sense, right? But here's the interesting part—scientific studies have found that acting kind toward others makes us happier too.

When we know that we are doing something good and making life better for others, we feel proud of our behavior. This gives our brain a positivity boost—and also makes us more likely to be kind in the future. Everybody wins!

Want to do something good for others, but not sure where to start? Here are some ideas...

★ Keep an eye out at school for kids who look lonely or unhappy. Sometimes a friendly hello can make someone's day.

★ Offer to help your parents with tasks that need to be done around the house.

★ Raise money for a charity by having a bake sale, a sponsored swim, or anything you like!

Ask your parents to help you care for the animals in your area. You could plant flowers that bees can use to make honey, make a "bug hotel" for insects, or put out food for birds to eat.

Be kind to yourself

Sometimes we can be really kind toward other people, but really mean to ourselves!

Imagine if you had a friend who kept saying nasty, untrue things to you, like you can't do anything, you're not good enough, or people don't like you. You wouldn't want to keep them as a friend, would you?

But most of us know what it feels like to hear that mean voice inside our own head, and we seem to put up with it more when it comes from ourselves.

It's really hard to be happy and try our best when we have these negative thoughts bouncing around inside our brain. So it's important to think about how to be a better, kinder friend to yourself.

The next time you have nasty, negative thoughts about yourself and all the things you think you can't do or don't deserve, write them down on a piece of paper.

At the top of the page, write the name of someone you really like and care about. Imagine you're saying all of these horrible things to them—you never would, would you? How do you think it would make them feel if you did?

The fact that you're saying these things to yourself doesn't mean they hurt any less than if you said them to someone else. So on the other side of the page, write yourself a letter saying sorry for thinking all those mean things.

In your letter, write some positive things to yourself instead. Think about what you try hard to do, and tell yourself how proud you are for making those efforts.

KEEP THINKING POSITIVE!

Read through these positive-thinking tips
any time you need a quick reminder!

List your negative thoughts and try to find a
positive thought or action for each one.

Rather than seeing situations as all good or all bad, picture a scale and
think what you can do to push things further toward the "good" end.

When you make progress, take a moment to celebrate how hard you've worked!

Write things down you're thankful for
regularly, and then look back over them.

Find ways to make yourself smile and laugh,
to release happy chemicals in your brain.

Tell a trusted adult if something is really worrying you. Thinking
positive doesn't mean pretending everything is fine when it isn't!

Don't let annoying little things spoil your
day. Take a deep breath and move on!

If you're not sure why you feel negative, talk with a trusted
adult about what you're afraid might happen.

Visualize yourself making
positive changes and take
steps to make this a reality.

If other people's constant
negativity makes you feel
bad, talk to them about it.

Do kind and helpful things for others, whether it's
your friends, family, animals, or the planet.

Don't be mean to yourself! Talk to yourself kindly,
like you would to a friend.

Glossary

attitude A way of thinking or feeling about something, which often affects how you act

fixed mindset If you are using a fixed mindset, you believe that your intelligence is fixed and can't be changed

growth mindset If you are using a growth mindset, you believe that your intelligence is always changing because your brain can grow stronger

neurons Cells in your brain that pass information back and forth to each other

visualization Picturing something in your mind that you would like to come true in future

Index

Notes for adults

The concept of a "growth mindset" was developed by psychologist Carol Dweck, and is used to describe a way in which effective learners view themselves as being on a constant journey to develop their intelligence. This is supported by studies showing how our brains continue to develop throughout our lives, rather than intelligence and ability being static.

Responding with a growth mindset means being eager to learn more and seeing that making mistakes and getting feedback about how to improve are important parts of that journey.

A growth mindset is at one end of a continuum, and learners move between this and a "fixed mindset"—which is based on the belief that you're either smart or you're not.

A fixed mindset is unhelpful because it can make learners feel they need to "prove" rather than develop their intelligence. They may avoid challenges, not wanting to risk failing at anything, and this reluctance to make mistakes —and learn from them—can negatively affect the learning process.

Help children develop a growth mindset by:

• Giving specific positive feedback on their learning efforts, such as "Well done, you've been practicing…," rather than non-specific praise, such as "Good effort" or comments such as "Smart girl/boy!" that can encourage fixed-mindset thinking.

• Sharing times when you have had to persevere learning something new, and what helped you succeed.

• Encouraging them to keep a learning journal, where they can explore what they learn from new challenges and experiences.

• Trying to use positive, action-focused language with them, while still making it clear that you don't expect them to be happy all the time. The aim is to avoid feeling stuck in bad feelings rather than not expressing them at all.